Paola Amadesi

GHOSTS

(Caravaggio and Beatrice)

I

Rome, September 11, 1599.

A blinding sun.

A city infested with heat, torrid, unhealthy heat.

He looked around, looking for a way out, first with his eyes, then with his body.

Trapped in the crowd.

Impossible to move, to move even a few centimetres. Impossible.

Yet he did not want to see.

-Orazio - He whispered. But his voice almost did not come out, as in a nightmare in which we want to scream for help, but our voice is not there, drowned in throat. - Orazio. -

Nothing. He resigned himself. He turned to look at his friend who held his daughter close to his chest to shield her from people and horror, but his hand was unable to pull the man's robe.

Then he saw. And he didn't want to.

The sword glowed arrogantly. Insulted her, provoked her. And she was tired, too tired and sore, to accept even more provocations, to continue the battle, the endless war.

She looked at Lucrezia, who could no longer see her. Blinded by terror and shame, she squeezed her legs to keep from dripping the yellowish liquid that would have decreed her fear. She squeezed even tighter. Someone pushed her down, to meet the wooden support for her head. The girl turned her eyes to nowhere, not to see. Not to know.

Then, the voices of the men brought her back to that infamous moment and she instinctively turned around: Lucrezia was unable to force her large breasts onto the wooden table waiting for her end.

The girl tried help her, as if she, instead of coming face to face with death, found herself once again doing housework with her stepmother. Once again together, once again united by the same case. Malign, ominous, infernal. Here, yes: infernal. Like that unbearable heat, full of moisture rising from the fetid river.

Perhaps the sword hadn't made a sound. Or, perhaps, she had looked the other way. The fact is that, when she returned to cast her eyes on the gallows, Lucrezia's head was already useless and helpless.

A vacant look, a twisted mouth. She was now useless, no longer part of the world. Beatrice turned without tears and looked for Giacomo. Even with her hands tied she managed to touch him on the chest. Her voice was low but clear.

- Forgive yourself, because God has forgiven you, my love. We'll meet again. - And she kissed him.

- Orazio, God! - He cried aloud. Uselessly. Like a puppet without a voice of its own, without anyone to support it. - Orazio! Let's leave! - He was overwhelmed. His will totally helpless, futile. His will, which had always supported him. He could still see his friend not far away, but the man kept his eyes fixed in front of him and paid no attention to him. - Orazio, the little girl! Shit, take the baby away!!!! - Nothing. A faint echo that was dispersed among humanity infused with blood, martyrdom, a justice that did not belong to anyone.

He walked backwards, regardless of who was there.

He pushed, tugged, until he managed to get away a little. He saw that his friend did the same, and had put his hand to cover the eyes of the child. If he would have had a god, he would have thanked him. He was suffocated.

Beatrice advanced towards the bloody wooden plank of her stepmother's beheading. Dirty, wet, soaked in blood. Mastro Titta approached her, holding his hand towards her neck. The girl looked at him hard, as she had never looked at anyone. Maybe not, maybe she had looked at "him" like that, even if he was going to die. She tore off her veil that she wore around her neck, with her own hands.

She ordered the executioner not to approach, and she did so silently, with the only strength of her endless eyes. Without forgiveness, not even for herself. Without extenuating circumstances, or illusions. She also looked at the friar who understood and approached her. She kissed the wooden crucifix that the man was now offering her, and she accepted a belated yet necessary blessing.

- Amen. –

He couldn't have heard that whispered word. So short, intense, magical. *Amen.* Yet it went down into his stomach.

-      Michele! - His name, perhaps. He hardly remembered it anymore. Nothing made sense anymore, much less just any sound.

The girl looked down and spoke no more.

The sword hissed.

The body was still moving, without its head. It winced, didn't stop claiming life.

He didn't even know he had a life anymore. He heard a cry and turned: someone had fallen into the Tiber, pushed by the crowd, by delirium, by that unbearable heat.

He saw the young woman's head roll.

Then she was grabbed and placed next to her stepmother's.

Too big eyes now stared at him.

Giacomo felt ill, collapsed on his knees. Waiting for his execution.

-       Michele! -

- Orazio! -

He was free. The crowd was a little more distant, he was able to move his legs, even accelerate his pace towards his friend. Who went to meet him, out of breath. The little girl freed herself from her father's grasp and she walked towards him.

- Artemisia! - He shouted, kneeling to welcome her - Artemisia ... -

And he wept.

He cried.

II

He was sick.

He couldn't sleep, his eyes were tired and prevented him from painting.

Curse. Finally the important commissions and he could not work.

He rolled over in bed.

He dozed off, like a grace received when he no longer hoped for it.

The dream was clear, golden with a diaphanous light, in which the girl walked.

He looked at her, she smiled at him. Then she began to cry and fold her hands in prayer.

He reached out for touching her, but she was swallowed by a huge, scary dark hole. Then, from that same chasm, the girl's head rose, bloody, horrible to see. Her body, trapped in the pit, squirmed.

He leaned out: she was screaming. Her words were at first incomprehensible, then they became clearer: "I suffered," said her voice. "I suffered so much".

Michelangelo jumped out of his bed.

His throat burned, he looked for the pitcher. He clung to it furiously. His liquid dripped from his lips to his chin and into his chest. In that heat, he was fine. He wiped with the sleeve of his shirt.

He went out.

He didn't even know what he was looking for. He wandered around trying not to be recognized.

Without thinking, he took the road to his friend's house and knocked.

The little girl stood behind the heavy door, and she was meowing incomprehensible words.

He, from outside, whispered: - Artemisia, please call dad. -

He heard the small footsteps echoing between the walls and the high ceilings then, together with those of the child, he heard the heavier and more adult ones of her father.

- Caravaggio! - Orazio smiled, welcoming. - Come inside. -

He turned and preceded his friend towards the room that served as a study and as bedroom. He took a pitcher of wine, placed it on the table in the centre of the room. He added two mugs, moved the chairs.

- What's going on, Michele? - He asked pouring the wine.

The other shook his head. - I do not know. - He answered. - I have not slept anymore, since we saw the execution of the Cenci. -

-      Bad thing. I won't take Artemisia to see some things again. -

- Listen, Gentileschi: do you know if there are any of them still alive? -

- A brother, I think. In jail, of course. Why?...-

-      I do not know. - He grabbed the mug and emptied it. He had nothing more to ask or say. He got up, stroked the girl's head and went out.

Orazio would have forgiven his rudeness.

III

A long, deep shiver lay on his neck like a raptor.

And the further he went down the stairs, the colder the thrill became.

The jailer glared at him as he opened the cell door. He almost slammed him in as if he were a prisoner too, rather than a visitor.

Lying in the dark, on the damp and filthy pallet, the boy held his arm over his eyes, so as not to see what was around him.

He couldn't look, he had seen too much.

The guard shook him with his foot, the boy jumped. He peered into the dark and saw the man.

When the door was closed, Michelangelo approached him.

How old could he be? He was a kid.

- Messer Cenci, I'm Caravaggio. - He said softly.

The other sat down. - The painter? – He asked.

- The painter, yes. -

- What do you want from me? - The question had been uttered with haughtiness, a battered residue of his life as a noble.

- Just a few questions. I would like to meet your sister Beatrice. -

- You curse! My sister is dead! –

- I know, I know. But please tell me something about her: she prevents me from sleeping. I am sure that, if I knew, I would find peace. -

Bernardo looked at him as if he was mad, a different one. Michelangelo ignored that look. Without being invited, he sat down on the pallet and continued: -Let me meet her. I only saw her die, in front of the screaming and pain-thirsty crowd of others. He was too young, too innocent to die in that way. —

Those words had the effect of melting the soul of the young man, who wept.

- Do you want to meet Beatrice, painter? So all right. I will approach her to you, doing my best ... -

And he began to speak, in a faint voice.

IV

There had been all that blood.

Dark, sticky, mixed with hidden moods, coming from unknown anatomical ravines.

All that blood between her shapely, white legs.

Too white, offended by that dark red matter.

Then one last long breath and then she did not move anymore.

Ersilia Santacroce had died for her umpteenth pregnancy, in an attempt to give birth to another child.

Someone had blown out the candles and drawn the curtains. And put a sheet over the inanimate body.

The child had cried, then she had been carried away from the death chamber.

In the dark, she had smelled the smell of her mother fading little by little.

She had tried to free herself, kicking like a little animal but with every movement, she wasted energy without succeeding.

The door had slammed shut on her despair.

She would have never seen her mother again.

V

- This story begins with pain. And pain is a red thread that cannot be undone, sir ...-

Michele looked at the young man, caressed by tears as shiny as silk.

- Our father, sir, was called Francesco Cenci and he was ferocious as a wild beast. On the death of our mother, whom Beatrice never knew because she was the cause of her death, he married again. The woman you saw next to my sister, today in the hour of her passing away, was Lucrezia, his second wife. You must know, sir, that

Lucrezia was the mother of a child, which our father did not hesitate to put down. How, we never knew ... –

Michelangelo scratched his head, running his hand through his thick dark hair. In his mind, the images ran overlapping, as in his bloody canvases.

- Go ahead, if you can... - He whispered to the boy.

There was a long pause, in which Bernard swallowed the anguish. Then, Michelangelo heard his voice again.

- The fortress humid, cold in winter and hot in summer, especially in the evening, when its large walls gave off all the heat they had retained during the day. We were sick up there. Far from civilization, from life. Far from a little bit of humanity. I was a child but I remember everything. All. And God only knows if I would like to forget. But I cannot. Our father had taken us up there, after he had denied the wedding to Beatrice, not to pay her dowry. This was the reason that led him to make us prisoners of his narrow-mindedness, between the gray and very high walls of the fortress of Petrella. My sister was young and eager for life: she was almost going mad in that place, watched over by our father's guards. Lucrezia shared that rough existence and helped her endure. Then something happened: Beatrice had started writing letters after letters, to whom I don't know. However, I know that she was asking for help, I had heard her talking to Lucrezia. She was asking for help and to be released.

don't know how, but our father got those letters. The cursed dog's rage poured out on her: with the drool in his mouth he beat her, with his hands and straps... She was bleeding, he did not stop beating her ... and I cried ... –

VI

He closed the door, exhausted. He pushed a heavy trunk in front of it, fearing someone might get in, and pulled the bolt. Alone, he must be alone. He clung to the jug of red with his mouth: it tasted as vinegar, the heat had been too much during the day. He spat, feeling even sadder, without at least the comfort of the wine. He stuck the knife into the bread, tore off a piece and chewed it greedily. A sip of water and he lay down. No candle, just a moon blade from the skylight. It started to rain, he fell asleep.

The great walls had echoed with screams.

The children had tried to defend themselves by raising their small whitish hands to the blades and their hands were filled with blood. And the voices had become thinner, scratched with terror. The children had seen the mother scrambling over them and falling back over them with broken breasts, her heart almost visible in the torn flesh. Hands over eyes and face, to defend against blows. They had not been able to see their father dragging himself, mortally wounded, to their bed. A blood-coloured darkness had engulfed them in the oblivion of the centuries.

But she felt them. She wandered through corridors and large rooms with a sense of cold inside, loneliness and fear. She saw them, repeating the same macabre scene over and over again. She felt suffocated and ran out. Then she returned and, even if she pretended indifference, a prolonged shadow on the wall, any rustle, was enough to freeze her blood. She told Lucrezia who believed her: she too had seen something, but she couldn't explain what. They had asked the guardians, who had told them of the murder of the Mareri family by the hands of the son-in-law of the householder, who had broken a promise made on his daughter's wedding day: the concession of a castle. In addition, he had been accused of being the lover of his mother-in-law and had not tolerated any longer.

And behold, the avenging hand had exterminated the in-laws and little brothers-in-law.

Except Maria Costanza, who had saved herself because her rich dress had clung to an iron and had prevented her from falling from the fortress.

The fact had happened at the beginning of the century, right in there and Beatrice couldn't rest.

- Ghosts, painter. Damned deads who wandered without peace in that gloomy place. Already stained with dried blood, a cursed place. My sister saw them, those ghosts, she suffered with them, got more and more anxious. Gianfrancesco Mareri, so I later learned, had promised the castle of Staffoli to his son-in-law, Giacomo Facchini. But he did not keep his promise and Facchini took revenge: he allied himself with a victim of Mareri, a servant who had a brother killed by the count and at night he killed the whole family. Only little Maria Costanza was saved from her, because she, falling from the fortress, had her dress caught on an iron and saved her life. But her family had been exterminated. And her ghosts tortured Beatrice. And ghosts bring ghosts, painter....-

It was a pink dawn, which swelled the air with humidity.
The Tiber was turning red and he was exhausted.
The day was beginning and the young Cenci would be taken to the papal galley to serve the sentence of the eternal oars.
If he was lucky, and Bernard hadn't gone on a long trip in a galley, he would have found him in his cell on the night that would come.
He threw himself on the bed, to fight against his personal ghosts.

- He is a child, Gentileschi. And he talks like an old man. His words are drenched in pain. He is ashamed for the collapse of his family. There is something that he has not told me yet: if the girl was guilty of the paternal murder, she must have had a serious reason for committing a crime that was certainly suffered so much ...-
Orazio cleaned the brush with a rag already soaked in colours, which the dried varnish had made hard and dry as leather. He wiped his hands on the front of his shirt and went to the fire to stir the soup. -
- Caravaggio, if you continue to macerate yourself in this story, you will fall ill. -
Gentileschi's smile was as comforting as a hug. It was what Michelangelo needed. Like him, he as well needed that hot soup that his friend put in front of him. He grabbed the spoon and filled his mouth with it.
- Eat slowly, it's hot. - The other suggested.
He shook his head.
- It doesn't give me satisfaction to sip life, I have to swallow it. - He answered.
- The same you do with pain. Because tonight you will return to Tor di Nona, I guess ... -
The other nodded.
- That girl won't give you peace. -
Another assent with his head.

- You cannot avoid giving an answer to whoever calls you, just as you cannot avoid fate.-

Michelangelo pushed away the emptied bowl, crossed his arms on the table and rested his forehead on them.

A small child's hand caressed his hair. He jumped up. He looked at her and held her in her arms.

-Artemisia, Artemisia - he said softly - may your life be easy. -

While he was tidying up, Orazio was sure to see tears on his friend's face.

VII

Tor di Nona swallowed him again, with the steep and slippery stairs, the cold walls, paradoxical, at the mere thought of the external heat.

He felt swallowed by the cold, with a shiver of pleasure.

When she reached Bernardo's cell, the boy was exhausted.

He had bloody sores in the palms of his hands and swollen knees from the constriction of the galley's oars. And, fortunately, he had returned that evening.

Seeing him, Michelangelo thought that his young man, too young and slender body, would not have resisted that daily martyrdom, inflicted for the rest of his life.

-Bernardo ...- he said softly - If you don't want to talk tonight, I'll go away. -

The boy got up painfully from his bed.

He held out his skinned hand to the painter.

- No, Caravaggio, stay! I was waiting for you. You are my only friend, even though I know you don't come here for me ... -

Something inside Michelangelo cracked him. He felt a painful sadness in his chest.

He sat down next to the boy. He instinctively gave him a caress on the badly shaved head of a violent razor, which had left wounds transformed into purulent scabs.

-I know what I have to tell you, painter, and I will. –

In the thick night, thick as thick fog, the door had opened to her intimacy. She instinctively gripped the blanket with her hands and mechanically brought it up to her mouth. Francesco had appeared at the foot of the bed as a nightmare. He had moved closer, his round eyes wide on her. His big hand had uncovered the girl's body and with the other had pulled up her night gown. Beatrice hadn't breathed a word terrorized.

Francesco had first desecrated her with his big and filthy fingers, to open a first passage, then opened her legs and entered in her bowels with blows of his kidneys indifferent to pain.

Beatrice had smelled his male scent as an herbivorous animal smells that of a carnivore.

And she was devoured.

- Do you understand, painter? My father, worse than a stinking boar, had pounced on her, sucked her childhood like a magpie sucks a dove's brain to kill it in a single moment. And do you know what he told her? "When I refused, he filled me with blows. He told me that when a father knows... carnally his own daughter, the children who will born will be saints, and that all the greatest saints are born in this way, that is, that their grandfather was their father ". We only knew later, all this, when there was ... the trial. But I'll tell you at the right time. Go now, come back tomorrow, I'll finish my story....–

He hated having "premonitions". And yet, despite his will, he had.
He "felt" that the following evening he would have not found Bernardo, but during the day he ignored that feeling that harassed him.
You should listen to yourself: the truth is already within you. -

Orazio told him when he found him in the tavern drunk with cheap wine.

-      Bullshits. I only know that the boy will not be there tonight and neither will tomorrow. And he won't be able to finish his story. Only this I know, not the truth.-

- It is a truth. -

- What do we know? Maybe I'm wrong. -

- You also know another truth. - Orazio looked at him enigmatic and direct.

- Beatrice's, you mean? He emerged from the glass.

-      Yes. -

- I know that the girl was looking for an excuse to kill her father and that, probably, she found it in his violence. Carnal or not, it's always about violence. Carnal or not, only she can know. And she is dead. -

- You will hear the end of Bernardo's tale.

- The boy knows what he has been given to know. And he drowns in hatred. But I'll listen to him. Because, if Beatrice killed her father, there must be a reason. And so much pain behind such a drastic fact. How many happen, but few by a girls' hand. A daughter kills her father. Usually, alas, it's the other way around. Fathers who massacre daughters according to their disobedience, considered unworthy to bear their name just because they may have fallen in love with a man not chosen by their father. And these atrocious gestures have always been forgiven, but that of an exasperated daughter cannot be forgiven....-

He got up, went out in the air.

He tried to breathe, but the humidity swallowed him again, taking his breath away.

That evening, however, a gentle wind had risen, which had dried the air.

Michelangelo smelled it as a good omen.

He headed for Tor di Nona, even though he knew he would not find Bernardo.

"Come back in three days," the guard told him: the young man was on his way to Naples in a papal galea. He would come back exhausted, he thought. Without the strength to speak, to finish that short-winded story, as he felt to be his while waiting for him. He sneaked into the air, finally fresh, of the night. Trying to breathe.

Here she is: so white, surrounded by white.

"When I was a child, I had the same dream every night. I was naked in an immense room and a beast breathes, breathes, never stops breathing. "

She rolled over in bed, her throat dry.

"I notice that my body is shining. I would like to escape, but I have to hide my naked body. "

She looked for the crumpled sheet, tore it off pulling it up to her crotch.

"Then a door opens. And she suddenly discovered that I am not alone. No! Along with the beast breathing beside me, other things seem to breathe; and suddenly I see a mass of filthy things swarming at my feet. And they are hungry too. I start running without stopping to try to find the light again. The beast, which pursues me, chases me from cave to cave, I feel it on me, it's hungry, very hungry ..."

He could hear her voice, perceived as real.

He was shocked.

He hadn't seen the features of her face, but it was her: Beatrice. What did she want to tell him? Was she guilty or innocent? Had she really been tortured in her body and spirit by her father? Or was her just a mass of lies intended to justify a criminal act?

VIII

Death, however.

He hadn't put his nose out of the door, not even when Orazio had knocked insistently. He had not gone to the cardinal, he had deserted life.

The search for life, which haunted him.

He waited for the milky sun to set, then went to the jail.

The ninth tower, the medieval grain deposit called Turris annonae, was filled with sinister cells on the bank of the Tiber.

Michelangelo placed a coin in the hands of the oarsman who would ferry him to the building, whose square shape crushed the passers-by threateningly, with its height and heavy bulk.

On the ground floor, small rotted wooden crates hung from the tiny slits of the cells, waiting for some good heart to place a coin to give the prisoners a living in the seemingly dormant stone giant. However, while getting closer, it was possible to hear more and more clear and piercing screams of agony of the prisoners. In the cells called "secret", men and women were tortured. The most fearsome was "La veglia", a room in which torturers were among the most refined, able to inflict excruciating pain on prisoners without making them die before full confession.

Michelangelo got off the boat and stopped.

He looked up and never wanted to: in the orange light of the torches swayed the bodies of the condemned killed and then hung from the battlements of the towers as a warning to the citizens.

He went through the door, passed the chancellery, the reception halls of the various authorities, the infirmary, and reached the cellar.

He bought two flasks of red wine, which he paid little, because the sale in prison was exempt from tax and therefore the goods cost less than in the tavern.

Then he went up the stairs and reached Bernardo's floor.

The boy was there, finally. He felt reassured. Not so much for the young man's safety, but for the possibility of satisfying the need to know about him. Bernardo turned his head towards him, hinting a smile that was slow in coming. The thin and bruised body was stretched out on the motionless bed. Michelangelo approached to him.

-       I'm here. - He whispered.

The other nodded. He closed his eyes. Michelangelo understood that he had to keep quiet and wait. He sat down on the ground, on the damp and filthy stone and waited. The boy's voice was as thin as such a tense thread of wool about to break.

- We agreed. - He took long breaks, caught his breath and grabbed unhappy memories. - Well, we agreed to kill our father. Giacomo and I, our mother and Beatrice. We tried with a glass of poisoned wine, but he didn't drink after smelling it. He locked at us up and beat but then went back to his business. Then we hired brigands who attacked him on the road, but the guards saved his life. So we asked for help to Calvetti, a castellan of our acquaintance, and to a farrier, Catalano. But I think he had another name that I don't remember at the moment ... –

Giacomo mixed the liquid with the powder like an alchemist, paying close attention to weights and measures, so as not to make mistakes. Nothing could be careless, casual, roughly done. A scientific attitude accompanied the boy's hands, still in anxiety. Not of pain but of fear. To be discovered, to be accused. Terror of punishment, not of the crime.

When he had finished, he poured the drink into a glass and walked down the hall. The night was silent, perhaps too quiet: his footsteps sounded disturbing to his own ears. At the door, he knocked lightly. His father's voice thundered from within. He entered the room and walked over to the leather chair his father was sitting on and handed him the glass. The man looked at him. Maybe better than how his sister would have been looked, Giacomo told himself, because he was a boy and could be trusted. *Canis canem non est*, Francesco told himself when he saw his son.

Taking his leave, Giacomo did not go to the exit, but to the curtain that divided the bed from the room environment, with one hand he moved the door but did not go outside: instead he took up position, breathless, unseen, to observe.

He made sure that Francesco's hand brought the liquid to his lips and that his mouth swallowed it. That his eyes became heavy and closed slowly. Then he went back into the corridor.

Outside, Marzio da Fioran, known as Catalano, looked at him expectantly and so was his friend from the castle Olimpio Calvetti next to him. The two men entered, Giacomo behind them. The farrier dosed the strength of his elbow accustomed to the big equine feet and struck two precise blows of the club to Francesco's legs, to immobilize him in the pain of the fractured limbs.

He woke up, opened his mouth wide but no word came out. Then Olimpio, avoiding his gaze, holding a big hammer, hit him on the head and had to turn his head not to be reached by the fluids of the dying man, which splashed everywhere, then, without losing his emotional and physical momentum, he stuck a big nail in the man's throat. Slaughtered like a pig ready to be slaughtered, Francesco died with his eyes open, staring at his killers.

- There was an investigation. - Bernardo continued. Michelangelo listened in silence. - It started by chance, because of the rumours about my father, his cruelty, his greed. His body was found on

November 9th last year, thrown in a garden under the fortress. We, after short and squalid funeral rites, finally returned to Rome. -

- So it wasn't your sister who killed your father! - Michelangelo felt relieved.

- No. But wait, painter: I still have to tell you something.

The woman was fumbling with her hands in the water, looking for a lost handkerchief. Under the sun, on his knees by the river, she swore through her teeth at the loss of precious working time. The man stopped behind her, obscuring the sun, the woman whirled around. He made her stand up taking her by her arm, the woman moaned softly. Then he dragged her away badly, she didn't know why. Then, in the presence of the soldiers, she was asked about a bloody sheet.

The washerwoman who had been in our pay for many years replied that Beatrice had given it to her to wash it. And she added that my sister had talked about her menstrual cycle, about her blood shed on that sheet, when she entrusted it to her. However, painter, the washerwoman said so with such doubtful expression that no one believed her... And then there was no blood around the corpse, when it was found under the fortress. And if there was no blood, it meant that the crime had not occurred in the place where it was found. The investigations then turned to Beatrice. It must also be said that Calvetti, under torture, confessed to the murder. He dragged us all to hell with him. And then, my sister....-

The rope pulled, stopped, kept pulling. Suddenly it loosened and pulled again. Beatrice, hanging from her wrists, felt them shatter, the pain increase, until her whole body was only ache. She had taken care not to show herself naked, when they had torn her clothes off then, as the disease had invaded every nerve, every muscle, she had stopped thinking about what now seemed nonsense. Her shoulders had given way immediately, the sprain gave her cold shivers. The man did not stop turning the pulley.
To stop and then start over. Perhaps he had looked at her with compassion, at first, now she could no longer see him, with all that pain in her eyes. Finally, she felt his body collapse to the ground, suddenly freed from the rope. Then the darkness, in front of the eyes wide open, the same darkness behind the closed eyelids.

- Beatrice could not help but confess! - Michelangelo jumped to his feet. - They tortured her, I had to imagine. Of course, that's why she has committed such a serious crime! -

He turned to Bernard, who kept his eyes on the infinite, damp ceiling. He wasn't breathing.

He took his head in his hands, raised it a little and saw that the boy gasped. He ran to the door and began to punch. He screamed loudly for the guard. When the door opened, he slipped out, annihilated by so much pain.

Who knows how long he had slept.

Maybe for a whole day, maybe more.

Upon awakening, he found on the table a bowl of soup and a half of red wine, accompanied by a scrap of paper: "I'll wait for you at home. Orazio. "

He smiled, sat down and ate heartily. He drank even more. Then he washed his face and went out.

- I got some information: the investigations were initiated by Moscato, considered a fair judge. The lawyer Molella brought forward the accusation against the Cenci, while Farinacci assumed their defence. - Orazio used to talk with his calm manner which gave Michelangelo calm and affection. - You must know that Beatrice has never admitted that she had been raped by her father. But it is also true that Farinacci was not allowed to deliver the final plea: he was expelled from the courtroom before the sentence. And this tells a lot about justice: the law should be the same for everyone, but not everyone is the same before the law. Ultimately, the pope wanted to set a striking example, to show an exemplary punishment for family violence: too many episodes annoy these times and the state. For which the Cenci were punished, whatever the truth was ... -

Michelangelo nodded through gritted teeth.

"Where is the girl?" He asked suddenly, already enraptured elsewhere by his fantasies.

Orazio turned and called her. The little girl arrived, her dress dyed in her father's colours. Michelangelo bent down to embrace her.

"I'm taking Artemisia out," he said.

Orazio smiled.

Michelangelo and the little girl set off along the river.

The October leaves chased their steps, like light souls.

And like light souls they touched the heart and slipped away with an imperceptible rustle, like ghosts in the evening air.

This story is part of "Ghosts" a tales collection, to which it gives its title, available on Amazon.

It has been translated by the author.

paola.amadesi@libero.it